A Big Bed for Jed

by **Laurie Friedman**

pictures by **Lisa Jahn-Clough**

Dial Books for Young Readers 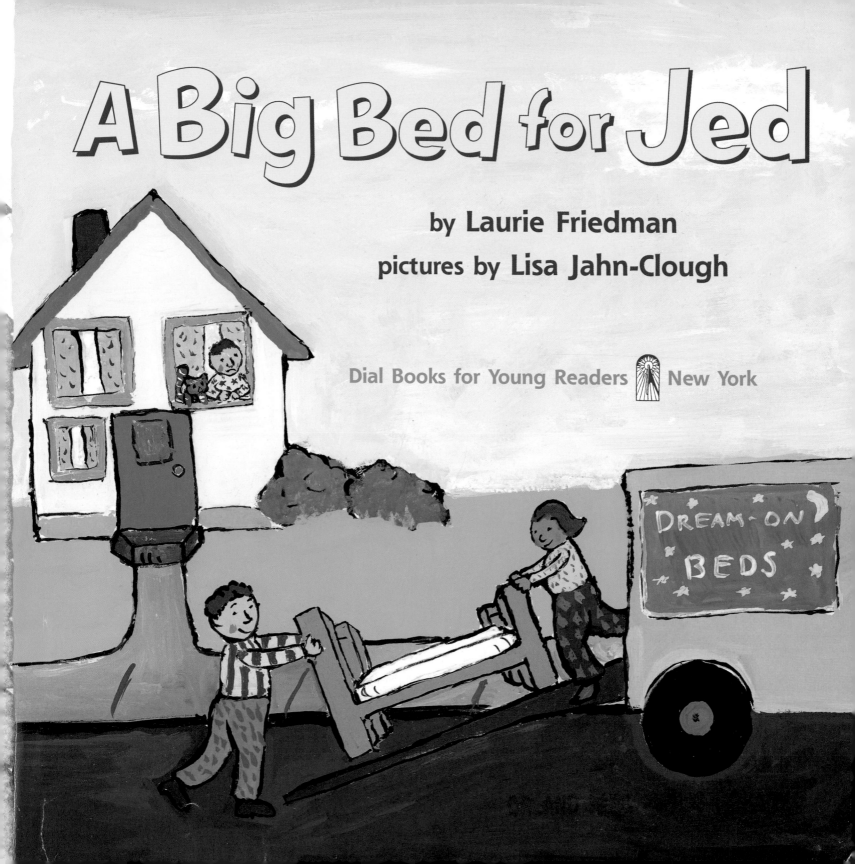 New York

DREAM-ON BEDS

**To Becca and Adam, who've always
made bedtime lots of fun
—L.F.**

**For James
—L.J-C.**

Published by Dial Books for Young Readers
A division of Penguin Putnam Inc.
345 Hudson Street
New York, New York 10014
Text copyright © 2002 by Laurie Friedman
Pictures copyright © 2002 by Lisa Jahn-Clough
All rights reserved
Designed by Lily Malcom
The text for this book is set in Shannon
Printed in Hong Kong on acid-free paper
1 3 5 7 9 10 8 6 4 2
Library of Congress Cataloging-in-Publication Data
Friedman, Laurie, date.
A big bed for Jed/by Laurie Friedman; pictures by Lisa Jahn-Clough.
p. cm.
Summary: When Jed is reluctant to move from his crib into a big-kid bed,
his entire family comes up with a plan to make him change his mind.
ISBN 0-8037-2562-0
[1. Beds—Fiction. 2. Stories in rhyme.] I. Jahn-Clough, Lisa, ill. II. Title.
PZ8.3.F9116 Bi 2002
[E]—dc21   99-057831

The full-color art was prepared using a pen line and gouache.

Jed loved his crib.
It felt just right.

Till his family surprised him
with a big bed one night.

"It's here!" said Mom.
"The bed that you chose.
Are you ready to try it?"

Jed just froze.

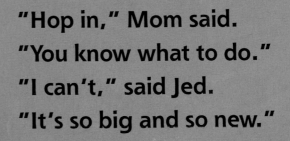

"Hop in," Mom said.
"You know what to do."
"I can't," said Jed.
"It's so big and so new."

"You've grown," said Dad.
"Your crib is too small."
"I'll fall out," said Jed,
"and roll down the hall!"

"Not with these," said his sister.
"They match your hair."
"I only like blue," said Jed,
"EVERYWHERE!"

"Here's something for you,"
said Jed's Auntie Stella.
"We think you'll love it
now that you're a big fella."

"There's more," said Uncle Stan.
"New pillows and a spread."
"There's no room," said Jed.
"We can't fit in this bed."

"Nonsense," said Dad.
"Now, not one more peep."
Dad phoned up Grandma.
"Jed won't go to sleep!"

Grandma rushed over
and she picked up Jed.
"Dear grandson," said Grandma.
"PLEASE GET IN THAT BED!"

NO NO

NO

Jed crossed his arms.
"I WILL *NOT* GO!"
He crawled under his crib
Yelling, "NO! NO! NO! NO!"

"Move the crib," sighed Dad.
   Grandma rolled it out the door.
   Mom threw up her hands.
"I can't take anymore!"

WAIT!

"We give up!" said Aunt Stella.
"We're leaving," said Uncle Stan.
"Wait!" yelled Jed's sister.
"What we need is a plan."

As they started to whisper,
the group drew in tight.
Whispering *psst, psst, psst* . . .
Till their plan was just right.

"Sweet dreams,"
yawned Uncle Stan,
"I'm going to sleep."
Then he slipped in Jed's bed
and began to count sheep.

Auntie Stella climbed in
and started to snore.
Jed's sister jumped in
and Grandma made four.

Mom and Dad got in last
and mumbled, "Good night."
"Dear Jed," whispered Grandma.
"Please turn out the light."

"BUT THAT'S MY BIG BED!"

And there wasn't a doubt.
Now that they were all in,
Jed wanted them OUT.

"*Sshh*," said his sister.
"We're trying to sleep."
"Keep it down," said Uncle Stan,
"you'll wake up the sheep."

Auntie Stella let out
a great snort and a snore.
And Dad said, "Well, Jed,
I guess you get the floor."

Jed started to think.
Now what could he do
to get them all out?

And suddenly . . .
he knew!

Jed bounced on his sister.
He sat on his dad.
He rolled on his grandma.
Mom cried out, "E-GAD!"

E-GAD!

He tossed up the pillows
and hid under the sheet,
and they all squirmed and giggled
when Jed tickled their feet.

Especially Aunt Stella,
who hollered, "What fun!"
As Uncle Stan led them out
of the bed, one by one.

Then Jed pulled up the covers
of his great big new bed.
"See you in the morning,"
was all that he said.

He got lots of kisses
and lots of good-nights.
It was bedtime at Jed's.

Mom turned out the lights.